BAD APPLE's
Perfect Day

written and illustrated by
Edward Hemingway

G. P. PUTNAM'S SONS • **An Imprint of Penguin Group (USA)**

For Coco and Steve Kirchhoff

G. P. PUTNAM'S SONS
Published by the Penguin Group
Penguin Group (USA) LLC
375 Hudson Street, New York, NY 10014

USA | Canada | UK | Ireland | Australia | New Zealand | India | South Africa | China
penguin.com
A Penguin Random House Company

Library of Congress Cataloging-in-Publication Data
Hemingway, Edward, author, illustrator.
Bad Apple's perfect day / written and illustrated by Edward Hemingway.
pages cm
Summary: Mac the apple and Will the worm set out for a perfect day at the watering hole,
and although little goes as they plan, friendship, imagination, and a sense of fun make everything turn out fine.
[1. Apples—Fiction. 2. Worms—Fiction. 3. Friendship—Fiction.] I. Title.
PZ7.H377436Bbm 2014 [E]—dc23 2013017564

Manufactured in China by South China Printing Co. Ltd.
ISBN 978-0-399-16036-3
1 3 5 7 9 10 8 6 4 2

Design by Ryan Thomann.
Text set in Metallophile, Mushmellow, and a bit of Ad Pro and Carrotflower.
The art was done in oils on canvas.

The sun was rising.
The crickets were chirping.
And Mac and Will were getting ready
for the perfect day.

Mac couldn't wait to go to the watering hole.
On a sunny day, there was no better place to be.

Today I will show you my . . .

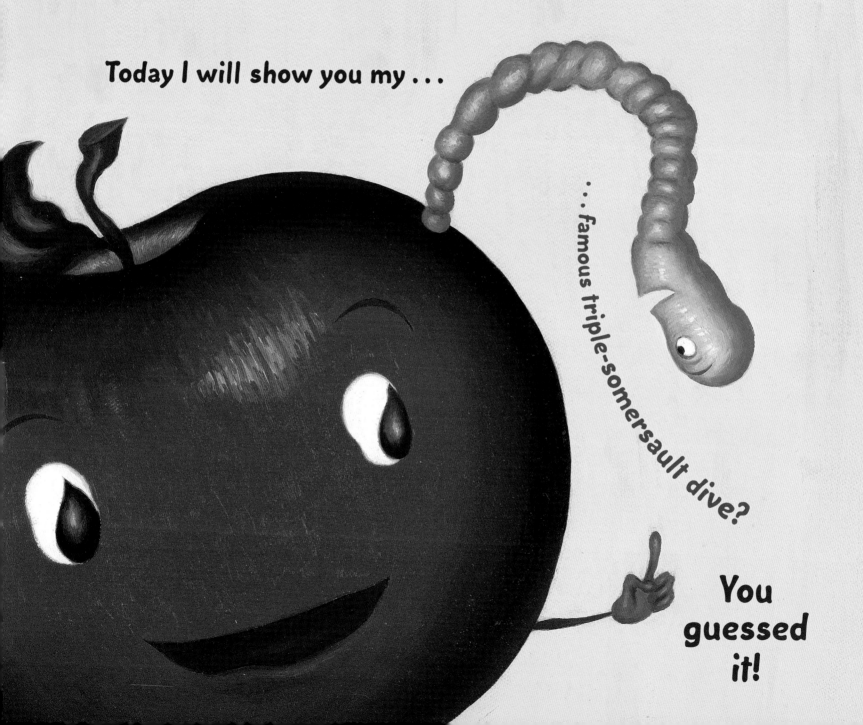

. . . famous triple-somersault dive?

You guessed it!

It was a short trip
if you traveled light.

But the watering hole hadn't seen rain in ages, just some sour apples.

Still, Mac and Will were determined to make the most of it.

SPLAT!

HA! HA!
LOOK AT THE BAD APPLE!

BAD APPLE?
HIS NAME IS MUD!

Mac felt a little silly,
but Will hated to waste
perfectly good mud.

It wasn't long before their friends dropped by

and the crab apples dropped in!

Behold, the Amazing City of Mud!

But before they could finish their city, it began to rain . . .

RUMBLE!

and thunder started to roll.

Some perfect day
this was turning out to be.

Luckily, it's never too late to turn things around.

On rainy days, a little voice
in my head tells me to . . .

. . . read a book? Too bad we don't have any.

True, but we don't
need a book to . . .

. . . tell a story!

So Mac began.

"But then clouds covered the sun and rain filled the sky. They got pretty wet hightailing it out of there."

"They built a bigger city—one that was taller than all the rain clouds in the world. It was very beautiful, and they were happy.

"And on top of the world!

"They realized that there was no limit to where they could go."

So who wants to tell . . . . . . the next story?

When the rain was down to less than a drizzle, the group made their way back to the watering hole and the Amazing City of Mud.

But it was gone.

There was nothing left to do except . . .

The double-barreled belly flop!

Wheee!

And the yellow-bellied leap of terror!

Eeek!

How do you like them apples?

Bobbing among friends, a tired and happy Mac
and Will couldn't think of a better place to be.

It was the perfect ending
to the perfect day.